Katie's Lucky Birthday

by Fran Manushkin

illustrated by Tammie Lyon

PICTURE WINDOW BOOKS

a capstone imprint

Katie Woo is published by Picture Window Books,
A Capstone Imprint
1710 Roe Crest Drive
North Mankato, Minnesota 56003
www.capstonepub.com

Library of Congress Cataloging-in-Publication Data
Manushkin, Fran.
Katie's lucky birthday / by Fran Manushkin; illustrated by Tammie Lyon.
p. cm. — (Katie Woo)
ISBN 978-1-4048-6514-3 (library binding)
ISBN 978-1-4048-6612-6 (paperback)
[1. Birthdays—Fiction. 2. Parties—Fiction. 3. Schools—Fiction. 4. Chinese Americans—
Fiction.]
I. Lyon, Tammie, ill. II. Title.
PZ7.M3195Kcl 2011
[E]—dc22   2010030658

Summary: Katie celebrates her birthday with her classmates.

Art Director: Kay Fraser
Graphic Designer: Emily Harris
Production Specialist: Michelle Biedscheid

Photo Credits
Fran Manushkin, pg. 26
Tammie Lyon, pg. 26

Printed in the United States of America in Stevens Point, Wisconsin.
112014   008606R

Table of Contents

Chapter 1

Birthday Talk

Katie's birthday was

coming. "I'm having a party

at school!" she told her

friends. "I can't wait."

"I know how you feel,"

said JoJo. "Birthdays are the

best!"

"My mom measures me
on my birthday," said JoJo.
"It's fun to see how much
I've grown."

Pedro said, "On my birthday, my dad makes me blueberry pancakes. My birthday is in August, so there are plenty of blueberries."

"There is no school in August," said Katie. "So you can't have a party at school."

"Nope," said Pedro. "I never do."

Chapter 2

The Big Day

The sun was shining on
Katie's birthday. Her mom
and dad gave her a bright
red sweater.

"Red is my lucky color!"
Katie said. "It means my
birthday will be perfect."

"I made a special treat for your class party," said Katie's mom.

"What is it?" asked Katie.

"It's a surprise," said her mom. "You'll find out later."

When class began, Miss
Winkle announced, "Today
is Katie's birthday. She will
be my POD."

"What's a POD?" asked Barry, the new boy.

"It means Person of the Day," said Pedro.

"Katie can start by leading the Pledge," said Miss Winkle. Katie led the Pledge in a nice, loud voice.

Katie was also the line leader at recess. "I wish it was my birthday every day," she said.

"Well," said Pedro, "you have 364 unbirthdays. Today is one of mine."

The twins, Ellie and Max,

said, "Our birthday is double

the fun."

"Double the fun?"

repeated Katie. She looked

at Pedro. "That gives me an

idea!"

During art,
Katie asked the
twins to help her
paint a poster.
"It's a secret,"
Katie told them.

"We're great at keeping
secrets," said Ellie.

"Except from each other,"
added Max.

"What are you painting?"
asked Pedro.

"Oh, nothing," said Katie.

Pedro laughed. "When
you say nothing, it means
you are up to something!"

Chapter 3

Party Time!

Finally, it was time for Katie's party. Her mom came with the special treat. The plate was huge!

"My mother is up to something, too!" said Katie.

The class gasped when

they saw the treat. It was

a giant rose made of

strawberries.

"It's red! My lucky color!"

Katie said.

"HAPPY BIRTHDAY KATIE"

was spelled out in blueberries.

"Blueberries! My favorite!"

shouted Pedro.

"Katie's mom searched

until she found them," said

JoJo.

"Now, it's time for another surprise," announced Katie.

The twins held up Katie's secret poster. It said, "Happy Unbirthday, Pedro and Everyone Else!"

Pedro couldn't stop

smiling.

The class sang "Happy Birthday" to Katie. Then everyone ate the strawberries and blueberries.

On the way home, Katie

told JoJo and Pedro, "My

birthday party was totally

perfect."

"For me too!" added

Pedro. "I felt like a POD."

"That's because you are!"

Katie said.

Then the three of them

ran home. It was triple the

fun!

About the Author

Fran Manushkin is the author of many
popular picture books, including *How Mama
Brought the Spring; Baby, Come Out!; Latkes
and Applesauce: A Hanukkah Story;* and *The
Tushy Book.* There is a real Katie Woo — she's
Fran's great-niece — but she never gets in
half the trouble of the Katie Woo in the books.
Fran writes on her beloved Mac computer in New York City,
without the help of her two naughty cats, Gilda and Goldy.

About the Illustrator

Tammie Lyon began her love for drawing
at a young age while sitting at the
kitchen table with her dad. She continued
her love of art and eventually attended
the Columbus College of Art and Design,
where she earned a bachelors degree in fine
art. After a brief career as a professional
ballet dancer, she decided to devote herself full time to
illustration. Today she lives with her husband, Lee, in Cincinnati,
Ohio. Her dogs, Gus and Dudley, keep her company as she works
in her studio.

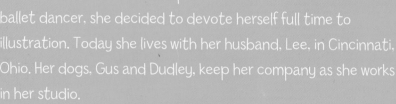

Glossary

announced (uh-NOUNSSD)—said something officially or to a group of people

favorite (FAY-vuh-rit)—the person or thing liked best

gasped (GASPD)—took in a sudden breath in surprise

Pledge (PLEJ)—refers to the Pledge of Allegiance, a promise to be loyal to the United States and its flag

repeated (ri-PEET-ed)—said or did something again

Discussion Questions

1. When is your birthday? Do you like having your birthday then, or do you wish it was during a different season?

2. On Pedro's birthday, he always has blueberry pancakes. This is a tradition. Do you have any birthday traditions?

3. How does your classroom celebrate birthdays? Compare this to what Katie's class does.

Writing Prompts

1. Write a sentence or two to explain what an unbirthday is, according to the book.

2. Think about your last birthday. What did you do? Write a paragraph about it.

3. Make a birthday card for Katie. Draw a picture, and write a special message.

It is fun to celebrate a special day, like a birthday. People throw parties. They make special food, and they decorate. And it just isn't a party without party hats. Before your next party, make hats for all your guests. This project can be a little tricky, so ask a grown-up for help.

Make Your Own Party Hats

What you need for each hat:

- A large sheet of construction paper
- Scissors
- Stapler or tape
- Hole punch
- Elastic cord
- Glue, glitter, markers, stickers, feathers, ribbons, and other decorations

What you do:

1. Roll a piece of paper into a cone shape. Staple or tape the sides, and trim the edges for an even brim.

2. Punch two holes on the opposite sides of the hat. Cut a piece of elastic cord, about 12 inches long. String the cord through the holes, and tie it. You may also want to add a piece of tape over each hole for reinforcement.

3. Now it is time to decorate your hat. Use markers, stickers, glitter, and nearly anything else you can dream up. Make each hat unique, and personalize them with your guests' names. For a finishing touch, wrap a length of feather boa or ribbon around the bottom of the hat. Secure with glue or staples.

Now it is time to celebrate. Enjoy your party with one-of-a-kind party hats!

THE FUN DOESN'T STOP HERE!

Discover more at www.capstonekids.com

- 💜 Videos & Contests
- ❀ Games & Puzzles
- 💜 Friends & Favorites
- ❀ Authors & Illustrators

Find cool websites and more books like this one at www.facthound.com. Just type in the Book ID: **9781404865143** and you're ready to go!

E MANUS   YOU

Manushkin, Fran.

Katie's lucky birthday /

YOUNG

06/16